For Emily, with love ~ A.McA.
To Safi, the littlest Fish ~ T.B.

Clarion Books
a Houghton Mifflin Company imprint
215 Park Avenue South, New York, NY 10003
Text copyright © 2004 by Angela McAllister
Illustrations copyright © 2004 by Tiphanie Beeke
Published by arrangement with Macmillan Children's Books,
a division of Macmillan Publishers Ltd., United Kingdom.
First American edition, 2006.

The illustrations were executed in watercolor and mixed media.
The text was set in 19-point Venetian301 BT.

www.houghtonmifflinbooks.com

Printed in Belgium.

Library of Congress Cataloging-in-Publication Data

McAllister, Angela.
Brave Bitsy and the bear / by Angela McAllister ; illustrated by Tiphanie Beeke.—1st American ed.
p. cm.
Summary: A small toy rabbit and a large woodland bear come to each other's rescue during the winter.
ISBN-13: 978-0-618-63994-6
ISBN-10: 0-618-63994-2
[1. Toys—Fiction. 2. Bears—Fiction. 3. Winter—Fiction.] I. Beeke, Tiphanie, ill. II. Title.
PZ7.M47825Br 2006
[E]—dc22
2005029790

10 9 8 7 6 5 4 3 2 1

Brave Bitsy and the Bear

by Angela McAllister

Illustrated by Tiphanie Beeke

CLARION BOOKS NEW YORK

Little Bitsy fell out of
her girl's pocket in the woods
one autumn afternoon.

THUMP!

"Help!" she cried. But her girl didn't hear.

Bitsy looked around.
The trees were so tall. The woods were so quiet.
"I'm lost and all alone," she said, trembling.
"But I must try to find my way home."

So she set off, singing a brave song.

Bitsy had not gone far when she heard a . . .

GROWL!

A big brown bear stepped
out from the trees.
Bitsy hid behind her ears.

"Are you lost, little one?" asked the bear gently.
"Yes," said Bitsy. "I have to
find my house—it has a blue door."

"Well, I was on the way to my cave," said the bear.
"It's time for my long winter sleep. But climb onto
my back, and I'll take you home first."

They began to tramp through the
woods, but soon Bear yawned.
"I'm so very tired. But don't let me
rest or I'll fall asleep and I won't
wake up until spring."

So Bitsy sang him one of her
most bouncy, wide-awake songs.

12

When Bear's eyelids grew heavy,
Bitsy sang a marching song and drummed
with her heels to keep him awake.

When Bear sat down for
a snooze, Bitsy gave a loud
"TARANTARA!"
until he carried on.

At last, Bitsy saw her house
with the blue door.

"Thank you for bringing me home," she said.
Bear smiled sleepily. "Goodbye, my friend, good night."
And he shuffled wearily back to the woods
to find his cave.

That night, Bitsy sat on the windowsill,
thinking of her friend. Did Bear reach his
cave or did he fall asleep on the way?

"There was no one to sing and
keep him awake," she thought sadly.

Outside, snow began to fall thick and fast.

By morning, icicles
hung at the window.

"If Bear has fallen
asleep on the way to his
cave, he'll freeze under
the snow," thought Bitsy.
"I must try to find him."

So taking a ball of wool from the
knitting basket, she lifted the latch
and climbed out the window.

Then she tied the end of the
wool to the garden gate and set off,
singing a hopeful song.

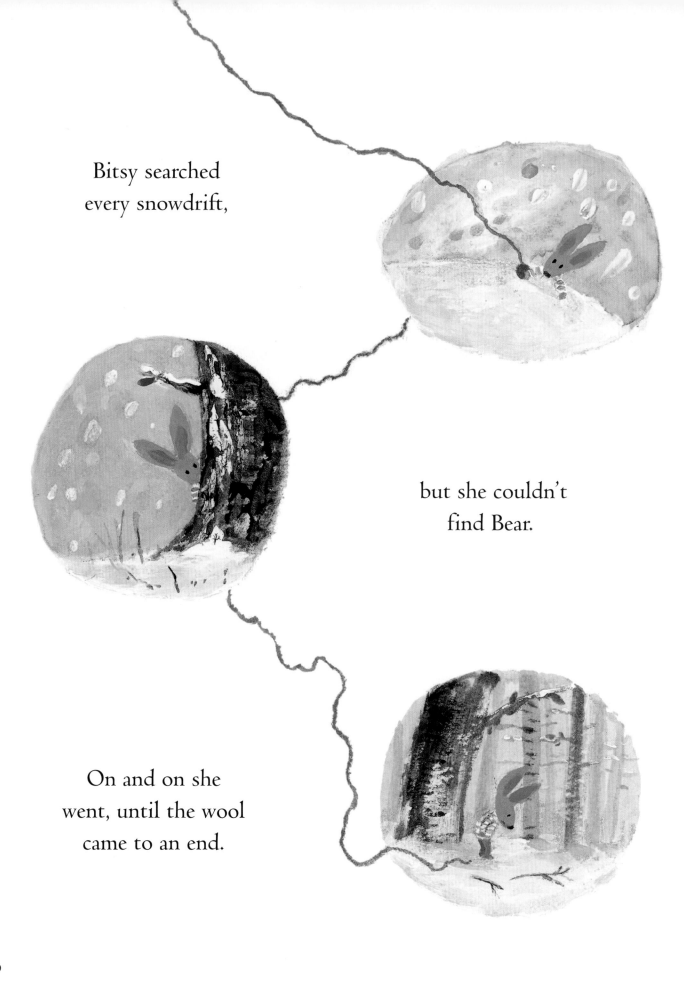

Bitsy searched
every snowdrift,

but she couldn't
find Bear.

On and on she
went, until the wool
came to an end.

She tied it to a loose thread
of her sweater and carried on.
"Bear, Bear, are you there?" she sang.
But no one answered.
Her sweater grew shorter and shorter.
At last, it unraveled completely.

Tired, and shivering with cold,
Bitsy could go no farther.
Just then, she heard a loud . . .

"SNNORGHH!"

And there was Bear, fast asleep with his head in his paws. Bitsy shook him. "Wake up!" she cried, and sang with all her heart, but Bear didn't stir. "He'll freeze unless I help him," she thought.

So she brushed the snow from Bear's coat and
tugged some bracken across his back. But the
wind blew it off and fresh snowflakes fell.

Bitsy hugged Bear's neck, but she had no warmth to give.

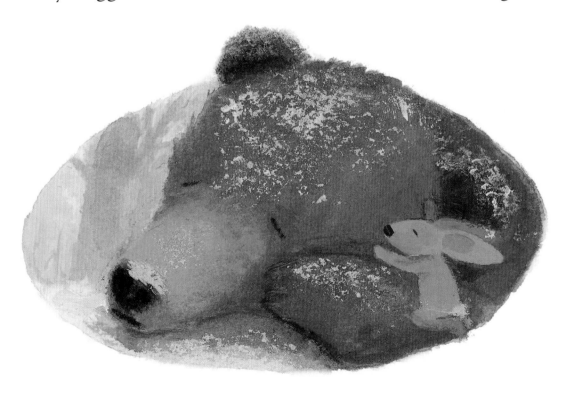

Then suddenly Bitsy heard a rustling
and a scratching. Out of the trees peeped
the creatures of the wood.

"We heard your singing, little rabbit," they said.
"We're Bear's friends, too. We can help him together."

The beavers built a shelter of wood.

The foxes fetched bracken,
and the squirrels brought moss for a blanket.

Soon Bear was warm again.

"Goodbye, my friend, good night," said Bitsy.

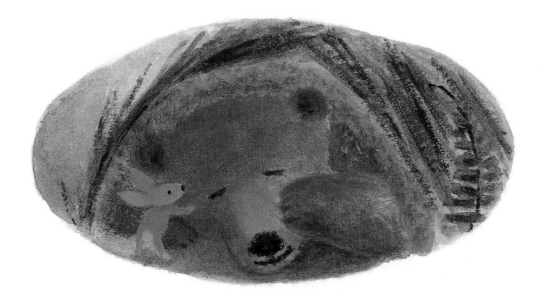

Then she followed the wool all the way home
and climbed back into her girl's cozy bed.

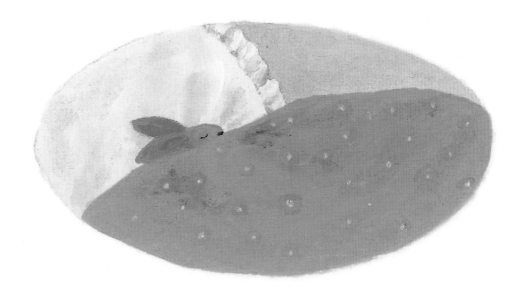

As she drifted off to sleep, Bitsy thought of
Bear under his mossy blanket in the snow and
hoped he would keep warm all winter long.

On the first morning of spring,
Bitsy ran to find Bear, singing her
sunniest waking song.

"Hello, little one," said Bear.
"Why, somebody made me such
a cozy bed. That was the best
winter sleep I ever had!"

Bitsy hugged him tight and smiled happily to herself.
And in the woods all around, Bear's friends smiled, too.